CW01425769

IMPOSSIBLE

DREAMS

PATI HILL

IMPOSSIBLE DREAMS

a novel

alicejamesbooks

138 Mt. Auburn Street, Cambridge, Massachusetts 02138

Cover photo: AMSON

A portion of the text of this book appeared in the Carolina Quarterly.

The publication of this book was supported by a grant from the National
Endowment for the Arts in Washington, D. C., a Federal Agency.

ALICE JAMES BOOKS are published by Alice James Poetry Cooperative 138
Mt. Auburn St., Cambridge, Mass. 02138

To My Parents

The photographs in this book have been processed to give them greater unity.

I would like to thank the photographers for their generosity not only in contributing their work but for the valuable encouragement and advice I received from them.

I would also like to thank Sylvia Lynch for her help at the time I was preparing the manuscript for the printer.

And, as always, the P.I.P. of New London.

IMPOSSIBLE
DREAMS

1

Although we live on the Boulevard St. Germain we rarely go to a café or even to a cinema.

My husband, Gérard, works for an American pharmaceutical company in the suburbs and when he gets home he prefers to watch télé.

Weekends, of course, we spend at our house in Melun or with my parents in Joigny.

In all fairness I should begin by saying I married well.

Gérard's father manufactured a well known brand of cough syrup until he died in 1960 and his mother inherited from her people who made *pain d'épice* in Dijon.

My own father is a second hand dealer.

(He is also an expert on 19th century engravings and my sister and I used to hope he would open a gallery in Paris. However, he claimed his health came from breathing country air and moving furniture.)

My mother was a hairdresser until she married my father.

As far back as I can remember she has been trying to bring order to the shifting contents of our house.

Gérard and I met at the Sorbonne.

The first time he asked me out I hesitated.

I knew he thought I would be easy to seduce because I lived in rooms instead of with a family. Furthermore I was in love with a boy named Maurice Grandin who had a face like a rat and got poor marks due to his gratuitous comments in class.

As it turned out Gérard was mainly interested in showing off his new car and Maurice quit school without leaving any address.

A few days after I went out with Gérard I visited my sister who is married to a bailiff and lives across the river from our parents in Joigny.

As we talked I was irritated by the way she kept moving about stirring this and folding that.

When we were children *I* had been the restless one.

"Never marry a poor man," she said, rapidly repairing the cord of the vacuum cleaner with flesh colored adhesive tape.

"I'll wait for Onassis," I promised her.

"What about going to Deauville for the weekend?" Gérard started asking.

"But no one goes to Deauville at this season," I objected.

"That's the point," said Gérard. "We'd have it all to ourselves."

"I have to visit my parents," I told him.

"I'll send you a postcard from the Casino," said Gérard, but when the day came he drove me to Joigny.

The weather was unusually fine and we ate on the terrace in spite of a keen wind that sprang up as we were putting on the tablecloth.

Afterwards we wound up an old gramaphone my father had bought at auction and played the records that came with it: Manon's *Adieu*, Schubert's *Marche Militaire* and *La Chanson d'Alain*.

Gérard's mother was not so quick to invite me as my family had been to invite Gérard and when she did it was only for tea.

Furthermore, the lift was out of order and we had to walk five flights to the top.

I was worried about perspiring and tried to slow Gérard up by getting him to kiss me as he often did on the stairs of my rooming house. He was not in the mood, though.

"You're so tall!" exclaimed Madame Bauve as we stepped in the door. "From Gérard's description I thought you'd be *petite*, but you're almost as tall as Gérard!"

HONNEUR AUX ARMES

GLOIRE A FRANCE COURAGE AUDACE

FIDELITE AU DRAPEAU FORCE ADRESSE

4e CORPS D'ARMÉE

BREVET DE PRÉVÔT D'ESCRIME

Accordé au Sieur Surgel

When it became obvious we would marry in spite of everything, Gérard's mother decided to give the reception.

My father arrived too early and stood in the middle of the room looking as if he was about to give a price on the lot.

My mother wore even more make-up than usual and invented a refined ancestry for herself.

Gérard gave me a pearl pendant, which I soon lost.

9

We were married under *séparation de biens* and spent our honeymoon in Lyons where Gérard wanted to visit one of his firm's installations.

I was poisoned by lobster (or the sauce, it was hard to say which) but in spite of this our son was born exactly nine months after our wedding night.

I wanted to call the boy Frédérique but Gérard preferred Michel.

He was born easily and had a happy disposition, yet I didn't love him.

Maybe it was because of the name. I don't think so, though.

If I believed in horoscopes I would say we were just the wrong signs for each other.

When Michel was five, Gérard inscribed him in the Woodrow Wilson Day School on the Champ de Mars.

I was proud that he was accepted because Woodrow Wilson School was hard to get into, but the idea of my child growing up speaking a foreign language troubled me and I delayed ordering his uniform.

The day before school was to open we went to the Grande Galerie where I hoped to buy something similar off the rack.

Michel loved the rolling staircase and insisted on riding to the top of the store before going to the boy's department.

As we were coming down again his toe got caught in one of the old-fashioned wooden grids.

A saleswoman saw the accident and quickly had the mechanism stopped, but it was nearly twenty minutes before it could be put into reverse and the toe released.

During this time Michel was very brave, gritting his teeth and rubbing his poor fists in his newly cut hair.

"It was my fault, Maman," he said as I held a paper cup of water to his lips, "*I* ran ahead of you. *I* made it happen."

"Be quiet," I whispered. "It was an *accident*!"

At the hospital Michel's toe was amputated and he was put into a room with a child whose head was entirely wrapped in bandages.

The next morning he was gay and we took him home where he complained that bad animals were fighting in the walls.

The following Monday his foot had to be amputated for gangrene.

"Why didn't you take him to the *American* Hospital?" Gérard wanted to know. "At the American Hospital nothing like this could have happened."

"Because I'm an idiot," I said. "Next time he catches his foot in an escalator I'll know what to do."

Of course we were both upset.

13

Michel died a few hours after the operation.

It was a blood clot and we were told he did not suffer at all.

I stayed home from the funeral because my mother-in-law was afraid it might give me a miscarriage.

To keep from brooding I cleaned out the top of the china cupboard and Laure was born that night.

From the moment I saw Laure I adored her.

She weighed only 5 pounds and the skin of her face was so transparent that you could see every vein, but she suited me perfectly.

(How strange I never mentioned being pregnant at the time of Michel's accident! All the while I was writing about it I was remembering how my bulkiness had made it difficult for me to comfort him.)

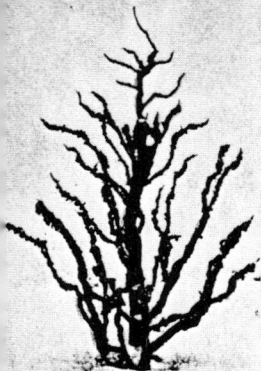

Laure's crying upset my mother-in-law so I spent as much time as I could in the park.

There I read *Le Grande Maulnes* and thought sometimes of Maurice Grandin. Not with regret, really. Just with wonder at the way he had come into my life and gone without our getting to know each other. Then it was cold and we went out only when there were errands to do.

In December the doctor told us my mother-in-law's fits of bad temper were due to an incurable illness.

Although I was not sorry at the prospect of losing my mother-in-law I did what I could to make her comfortable and in return she told me the girl Gérard had been engaged to marry before we met was neither so beautiful or so well off as she had led me to believe.

With Gérard's share of the inheritance we bought the apartment below us.

It had belonged to an old lady who died shortly before Madame Bauve and I often thought of the two of them looking into the courtyard where, if they were lucky, they got to see the concierge's dog relieving himself.

They might have enjoyed a few visits while they were still able to be wheeled about if they had not had a falling out some years previously. Over payment for a broken water pipe, I believe it was.

In the beginning Gérard planned only to paint and replace the worn sink downstairs, but after talking to some Americans at the laboratory he decided to buy furniture and remodel the kitchen as well.

I was surprised when he undertook to do the tiling himself.

The only work Gérard ever did at home was replacing blown fuses, but I didn't complain because it gave me time to read to Laure before putting her to bed.

Six years old already! But she still has all of her baby teeth and her fine silky hair.

I took it for granted we would buy furniture from father and I was looking forward to trading in the mahogany whatnot and one of our sideboards by the same occasion.

Gérard said everything had to be modern, however.

Well, I was foolish to get my hopes up. Gérard often criticized his mother's taste when she was living, but now she is dead it upsets him to change anything.

By the way," said Gérard, "I've hired a young lady to take care of the decoration. No point doing things half way."

The decorator came and went with Gérard's key so we never met though I often smelled her perfume in the hall outside the door. The same kind Gérard always gave his mother and me.

When everything was in order Gérard installed an intercommunication system between the bedrooms and the kitchen.

"But why?" I asked. "In an apartment that size you scarcely even need a bell."

"That's how much *you* know!" Gérard mysteriously replied.

The night before the rental agency took over I heard Gérard downstairs shouting, "Do you hear me? Tell me if you hear me," and Mademoiselle Dreux shouting back, "Yes, but not on the intercom."

Six weeks after the apartment was completed it was still vacant.

"Never mind," I said. "Sooner or later someone is bound to turn up who knows how to appreciate what you and Mademoiselle Dreux have down there!"

Gérard shot a glance at me, but I was bent over a jigsaw puzzle Laure and I had bought that afternoon at "L'Oiseau de Paradis."

(We keep a puzzle on the coffee table and in principle we only work on it when we are together, but sometimes I can't resist putting in a piece or two. Never anything important—just water or sky or foliage.)

One morning the agency asked if I would mind showing a client through the apartment myself.

I agreed on condition he come before midday, goodness knows why. I had nothing to do and the idea of showing the apartment amused me.

A man of thirty or so wearing one of the new Cardin suits rang my bell the following afternoon and I gave him a rapid tour.

As I was locking up he asked if he could bring his wife to look, too.

I told him he should call the agency for an appointment, but he explained that she was downstairs in the car.

I went back into the apartment and sat down on the new couch as if I were in the waiting room of Air France which, in fact, it slightly resembled.

Madame Ferrer wore her skirts up to her thighs and their little girl, who looked about Laure's age, was carrying a heavy cat.

Although there was something foreign about both Monsieur and Madame Ferrer I would not have guessed they were American if the agency had not told me, and the child pretended to be Chinese.

Monsieur Ferrer agreed to take the apartment on condition that we remove all the paintings and most of the furniture.

He gave as references the Swiss Icelandic Bank, the maitre d'hotel of a well known left bank restaurant and Madame Anna Schnable of La Celle St. Cloud who proved to have been his mother's maid in 1953.

"They sound rather dubious," Gérard complained. "We can wait."

However, as the agent pointed out, the only other offer had come from a manufacturer of reducing equipment who wished to use the space for demonstrations while his showrooms were being enlarged.

The night before the lease was signed Mademoiselle Dreux came to make out the inventory.

Although Gérard only went down for a few minutes, I could hear her typing until well past midnight.

Just as we were going to bed she telephoned and apparently asked about the inter-com because Gérard said, "Of course not! It's part of the electrical system," then sat for a long time brooding over his socks.

While Monsieur Ferrer read the lease I took a good look at Madame Ferrer across the new Danish table. table.

She was not quite so young as I had supposed at first and she wore thin gold hoops through the pierced lobes of her ears, which I disapproved of.

I suppose I thought that with ears that stuck out like hers she should have tried to cover them up instead of seeming so pleased with them.

Just as Monsieur was about to sign Madame Ferrer asked if the clock in the church facing the salon struck the hours.

Everyone was genuinely surprised and the agent said he did not believe clocks struck in Paris, only in London.

"What a pity!" said Madame Ferrer. "It would have been nice to hear the chimes!"

Mademoiselle Dreux couldn't (or wouldn't) get the stores to take back the unnecessary furniture so we rented a trailer and carried it to my father's place.

It was one of the first chilly days and he was piling apples into a copper bathtub in the courtyard.

"I can probably trade the boudoir chairs to la mère Bicoq for her feedboxes," my father told us, "but I prefer not to take on the paintings."

"Oh, I just brought them along for a friend," said Gérard.

While my father was inside showing some snuffboxes to an English couple Gérard asked me if I thought my father had refused the paintings to pay us back for buying new furniture.

I started to say, "Of course not!" then took pity and said, "Maybe."

After dinner we went with my sister and her husband to a bar to drink whiskey laced with anice, a thing we do occasionally in the same spirit that children put peanuts up their anuses.

My brother-in-law and Gérard do not have much to talk about except automobiles though they make surprising confidences to each other from time to time.

That night Gérard told Jean-Loup he had been a virgin when he married.

As we were undressing in the chilly bedroom where father had taken advantage of my years of absence to store a load of church benches, Gérard said suddenly,

"What if we went home? We could drive out to Melun tomorrow and see if there's anything up in the garden yet."

I said, "Laure will be disappointed. She likes to see her grandparents."

Gérard said, "Laure, Laure!"

On the way home Laure slept soundly wrapped in a blanket like the paintings and I thought about my life—how it was nearly half over and I had not yet done anything I cared to look back on.

Laure had a cold on Sunday so Gérard went to Melun alone.

He returned in a good humor and said the gardener was taking too many carrots and using too little fertilizer.

As I listened I realized he had not gone to Melun and was surprised at myself for thinking he would.

"Best not to be too hard on him," I said. "It's not easy to find a gardener these days."

I waited until he turned out the light to tell him that Madame Ferrer had called to say the new oven had burned out.

When I brought the electrician the next day Madame Ferrer asked if I thought he could glue back some of the tiles in the bathroom as well.

She was drying her hair and the child was drying the cat.

I don't believe I had ever seen a wet cat before. It looked all wrong, but I could hear it purring.

During the next few weeks I often saw Madame Ferrer and her child and sometimes an older man who had the same air of strolling about for his own pleasure that they had, even with their arms full of bundles.

Instead of short skirts, Madame Ferrer's costumes now dragged the ground which I found disturbing when we met in the dimly lit hall. They resembled so closely the period of our building that it was like seeing a ghost.

A person we never saw was Monsieur Ferrer.

In October Madame Ferrer called to say the oven was out of order again and ask if Laure could go to the Children's Circus.

"The performers are so beautiful," she explained. "All orphans or delinquents, and they never say a word."

I said I would speak to Gérard.

Gérard said, "Why not, as long as she's paying for the tickets?"

Laure surprised me by agreeing, too.

"I take the same bus Magali takes to school in the morning," she said. "She has a lunch box with riddles on it," she added after copying one or two more problems into her copy book.

Of course I shouldn't have been surprised. Laure leads a life of her own now. I just hate to be reminded of it.

While Laure and the Ferrers were at the circus I went to see a film called *Les Novices* with Brigitte Bardot and Annie Girardoux.

When I was in school I used to think Brigitte was the most beautiful woman in the world.

Now I prefer Annie Girardoux. She has character, though not in *Les Novices*.

When Laure got home she said, "Magali is selfish, I don't want to see her any more."

I said, "Eat your chop and you'll feel better."

Later I heard her crying in her room. I could tell by the way she stifled her sobs that she didn't want me to go to her, still I wished we weren't invited out to dinner at the Brells.

François and Chantal used to be our best friends in Sorbonne days, though they were more adventurous than we were.

When Chantal got pregnant she quit school and married François and they went to live in a rented room. Neither of their families would help them so Chantal took in typing.

Luckily François got a job at IBM the day he graduated and he did so well they sent him to Texas.

We went to the airport to see them off.

Gérard gave François a bright red tie and I gave Chantal a false diamond, and just as they were going through the turnstile Gérard stuffed a handful of confetti into François' mouth.

When they got back they played golf and bridge and took cruises on the Mediterranean.

On the rare occasions when we saw them they seemed wonderfully happy, so I was surprised when Gérard told me they were divorcing.

Chantal kept the children and the apartment in Neuilly and François went to live with Maryse Del-voye in a studio not far from where he and Chantal had started out.

Chantal and I lunch together fairly regularly since the divorce and she always manages to mention how it would never have happened if she had stayed home at Easter instead of taking the children to Brittany, but Gérard says this is not certain.

He says François was always unfaithful, even in their student days.

I said, "Why didn't you tell Chantal? Maybe she would have had a chance to keep him if she had known what was going on."

Gérard said, "It wasn't my affair. Besides why go out of your way to hurt somebody's pride?"

It hurt *my* pride the way François let us fall in their golfing days and took us up again after he married Maryse!

It was snowing when we left the Brells. Big shoddy looking flakes that wore out before they reached the ground.

In our courtyard we passed Monsieur Ferrer carrying a bulging canvas bag and something that looked like a parrot cage with a cover on it.

"It wouldn't be a parrot," I said as we drank Vichy in the pantry afterwards. "They have a cat."

"It would be all right if they kept it in its cage," said Gérard.

Neither of us felt like going to bed but there was no reason to stay up either.

I decided the best way to repay the Ferrers would be to invite Magali and Madame Ferrer to tea.

She said she could come any day except Tuesday when she planned to stay in bed and glue up photographs.

I suggested Thursday as that is the afternoon the children don't have school, adding that another day would be equally agreeable.

Thursday morning Laure and I went to look for a new bedspread like one she saw in *Elle Magazine* but they were sold out.

As we passed from department to department I was consumed by greed. For salt mills, brassieres, reading lamps. Even for atlases and crochet hooks.

As we returned through the Tuilerie Gardens I experienced a terrible nostalgia for the days when I used to walk Laure in the Jardin de Luxembourg.

We bought a *brioche* and a *chou à la créme* from the patisserie on the corner of the rue du Bac and the Boulevard St. Germain and Laure got out one of my mother-in-law's tea cloths.

I don't know if Laure is unusual. Probably at a certain age all girls begin to take an interest in the house. Laure even notices if the silver has been polished or a clean bath mat put out.

This encourages me to do things like keeping flowers on her night table, which irritates Gérard.

When the Ferrers weren't there by six I decided to call.

Madame Ferrer said, "Oh, I forgot . . . Will tomorrow do as well?"

I said, "Of course. It really hasn't the slightest importance."

I could hardly keep the irritation out of my voice!

"We often forget invitations," explained Madame Ferrer as I cut the *tarte aux pommes* which I thought was good enough for a Friday. "That's because we have so few."

I looked at her as Gérard had looked at me the other night and she smiled back showing her little irregular teeth.

While Laure and Magali played house in Laure's bedroom I learned that Madame Ferrer—Dolly—had been married three times, that she had gone to school in Geneva and that she ate only vegetables and fish.

"Did it go better this time?" I asked Laure when we were alone again.

Laure said, "It was all right only Magali doesn't have any actual Barbie dolls. And she uses a duck for the father."

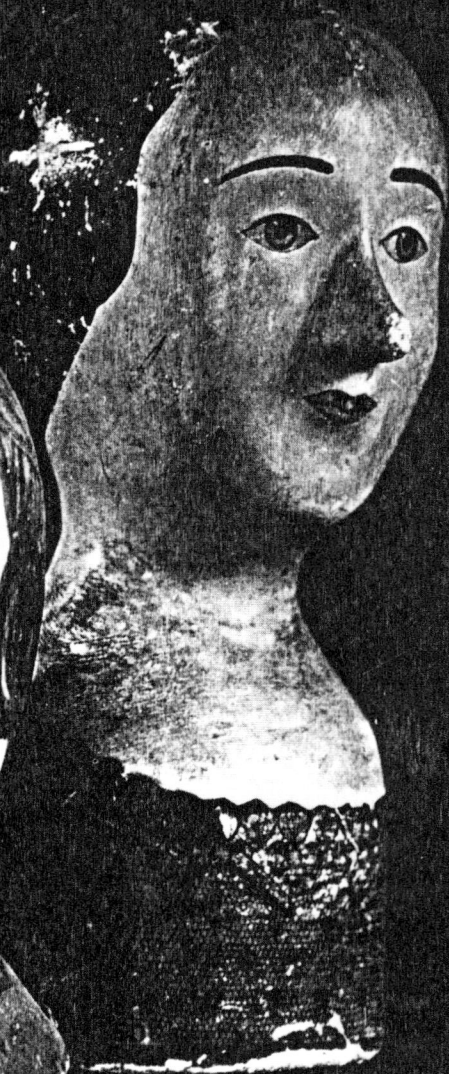

In November I took Dolly to see my sister in Joigny.

I thought they would enjoy each other but instead they seemed embarrassed as if they recognized each other but didn't want to admit it.

I took her to see my parents.

She asked the price of everything, even the bathtub where the apples were now swimming in rain water.

"You are furnishing a house nearby, perhaps?" my father suggested.

"What an idea!" laughed Dolly.

Gérard and I invited Dolly and her husband to a buffet supper with Maryse and François, but Monsieur Ferrer was away again and Dolly came dressed entirely in black.

She had even taken off the emerald she usually wore and spoke only in monosyllables.

"Dit-donc," said Gérard, after she left. "Our neighbor is rather glum."

I said, "yes."

I couldn't help imitating her.

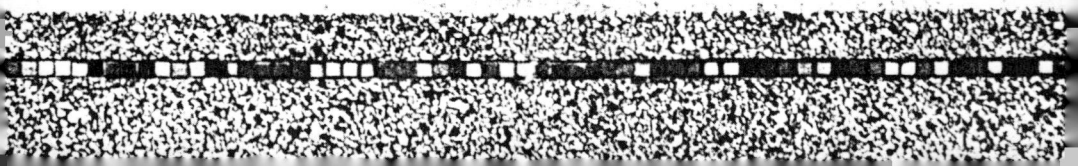

During the Christmas holidays Gérard and I usually take a châlet in Zermatt.

We do our own cooking and tidying and Laure sleeps on the couch.

I like the crowdedness and makeshiftness of it, maybe because we missed uncomfortable beginnings in our marriage, and I was counting on Zermatt to bring Gérard and me together. As the date came near it was evident Gérard did not want to leave Paris, though.

"Why don't you go with our tenant?" he asked one evening. "I'm too important to take winter vacations now."

Dolly accepted, then said, "What about Boris? Suppose he comes home for Christmas?"

I said, "Show him you can get along without him!"

Dolly said, "Why should I if I don't have to?"

I said, "Forgive me. I'm in a bad mood. If Boris turns up Laure and I will move to a hotel."

Magali and Laure wore their pajamas under their coats.

I packed sandwiches and Dolly brought fruit so we wouldn't have to stand in line for the diner.

The only other person in our compartment was an old lady who was already yawning before the train began to move so at nine o'clock sharp we switched out the lights and Dolly and the old lady talked until four.

"After all those years . . . . No social security . . . . Both of them better off that way too . . . ." and "How ironical! You did just the right thing . . . My aunt had the same experience," floated up to me.

The châlet was not the one indicated on the plan.

The arrangement was no different, but it was farther from the tow and next to a tavern.

Dolly never went outside except to scoop up snow to rinse her hair.

"Don't you want to get some exercise?" I asked when I had taken the children up the tow for a week.

Dolly said, "I got all the exercise I wanted when I was in school."

At night we mended socks and looked at the color television.

Just before we went home a couple of Austrian accountants invited us to dinner, but we couldn't find anyone to stay with the children.

Coming back there were no *couchettes*. We arrived at 7 in the morning, our faces stamped with plush and our feet wet.

At the control gate Dolly gasped and clutched her throat.

"My scarf! The one with all the colors! I left it on the seat."

As we waited for a taxi the children began kicking each others' boots in fun, then kept on in earnest.

To be truthful they did not like each other a great deal in spite of seeming to have been drawn together these past weeks.

The rubber plant was dead and the meal I had made for Gérard the night we left was still in the refrigerater, but the bed had been slept in and while we were having dinner Gérard asked me how I would like it if we spent next year in San Francisco.

I said "Goodness, Mademoiselle Dreux would take a week making the inventory if we rented *this* apartment!"

Gérard said, "That's all over. It wouldn't even be worth mentioning if you hadn't brought it up."

I said, "I don't know what you're talking about, I have to get the cheese."

Happily I had taken the trouble to buy some of his favorite Belgian Rocquefort.

62

"Let's have lunch at the Gare d'Orsay. They're
tearing it down to build a Hilton."

This is the note Dolly shoved under my door at
half past ten this morning.

It's out of the question, of course. The tinsmith is
coming to pick up the broiler at midday and I have
to cut out Laure's new dress.

I didn't even know the Gare d'Orsay *had* a restaurant.

"This building may not be the most beautiful in Paris, but it's the funniest and it needs protection," declares Dolly as we mount the marble stairs to the cloakroom.

She is dressed in her wolfskin, a red turtleneck turned over chin like a tongue, and hip boots.

I am wearing my raincoat because it is raining.

Below us are two groups of tourists, one Indonesian and one Swedish.

"First let me show you the men's room," says Dolly.

"But suppose someone's *in* there?" I protest. "After all this isn't a museum, Dolly."

"That's what's so wonderful about it," says Dolly. "You can really feel how things *were*!"

Dolly Dolly Dolly Dolly Dolly Dolly Dolly
Dolly Dolly Dolly Dolly Dolly Dolly Dolly Dolly
Dolly Dolly Dolly Dolly Dolly Dolly Dolly Dolly
Dolly Dolly Dolly Dolly Dolly Dolly Dolly Dolly
Dolly Dolly Dolly Dolly Dolly Dolly Dolly Dolly
Dolly Dolly Dolly Dolly Dolly Dolly Dolly Dolly
Dolly Dolly Dolly Dolly Dolly Dolly Dolly Dolly
Dolly Dolly Dolly Dolly Dolly Dolly Dolly Dolly
Dolly Dolly Dolly Dolly Dolly Dolly Dolly Dolly
Dolly Dolly Dolly Dolly Dolly Dolly Dolly Dolly
Dolly Dolly Dolly Dolly Dolly Dolly Dolly Dolly
Dolly Dolly Dolly Dolly Dolly Dolly Dolly Dolly
Dolly Dolly Dolly Dolly Dolly Dolly Dolly Dolly
Dolly Dolly Dolly Dolly Dolly Dolly Dolly Dolly
Dolly Dolly Dolly Dolly Dolly Dolly Dolly Dolly
Dolly Dolly Dolly Dolly Dolly Dolly Dolly Dolly
Dolly Dolly Dolly Dolly Dolly Dolly Dolly Dolly
Dolly Dolly Dolly Dolly Dolly Dolly Dolly Dolly
Dolly Dolly Dolly Dolly Dolly Dolly Dolly Dolly
Dolly Dolly Dolly Dolly Dolly Dolly Dolly Dolly
Dolly Dolly Dolly Dolly Dolly Dolly Dolly Dolly
Dolly Dolly Dolly Dolly Dolly Dolly Dolly Dolly
Dolly Dolly Dolly Dolly Dolly Dolly Dolly Dolly
Dolly Dolly Dolly Dolly Dolly Dolly Dolly Dolly
Dolly Dolly Dolly Dolly Dolly Dolly Dolly Dolly
Dolly Dolly Dolly Dolly Dolly Dolly Dolly Dolly

Dolly Dolly Dolly Dolly Dolly Dolly Dolly Dolly
Dolly Dolly Dolly Dolly Dolly Dolly Dolly Dolly
Dolly Dolly Dolly Dolly Dolly Dolly Dolly Dolly
Dolly Dolly Dolly Dolly Dolly Dolly Dolly Dolly
Dolly Dolly Dolly Dolly Dolly Dolly Dolly Dolly
Dolly Dolly Dolly Dolly Dolly Dolly Dolly Dolly
Dolly Dolly Dolly Dolly Dolly Dolly Dolly Dolly
Dolly Dolly Dolly Dolly Dolly Dolly Dolly Dolly
Dolly Dolly Dolly Dolly Dolly Dolly Dolly Dolly
Dolly Dolly Dolly Dolly Dolly Dolly Dolly Dolly
Dolly Dolly Dolly Dolly Dolly Dolly Dolly Dolly
Dolly Dolly Dolly Dolly Dolly Dolly Dolly Dolly
Dolly Dolly Dolly Dolly Dolly Dolly Dolly Dolly
Dolly Dolly Dolly Dolly Dolly Dolly Dolly Dolly
Dolly Dolly Dolly Dolly Dolly Dolly Dolly Dolly
Dolly Dolly Dolly Dolly Dolly Dolly Dolly Dolly
Dolly Dolly Dolly Dolly Dolly Dolly Dolly Dolly
Dolly Dolly Dolly Dolly Dolly Dolly Dolly Dolly
Dolly Dolly Dolly Dolly Dolly Dolly Dolly Dolly
Dolly Dolly Dolly Dolly Dolly Dolly Dolly Dolly
Dolly Dolly Dolly Dolly Dolly Dolly Dolly Dolly
Dolly Dolly Dolly Dolly Dolly Dolly Dolly Dolly
Dolly Dolly Dolly Dolly Dolly Dolly Dolly Dolly
Dolly Dolly rebounds from the four mirrored walls.

We cross a Sahara of groaning wooden waves, the waiter following with a towel.

"We'll have the Haut Brion '59, I think," says Dolly, pronouncing the 'H' good and hard."
"Ah, Madame . . . .
"A Château Fourgéon, then."
But there is no more Château Fourgéon, either, because to be truthful they have sold the cellar to a restaurant on the Quai d'Orleans, but there's a nice beaujolais and some warmed-over kidneys.

Now that the meal is taken care of I start looking for a subject of conversation worthy of so much space and so many cupids.

"I love you," I try out distractedly and Dolly replies, "I *knew* you would! But I can see how a Hilton might be more useful here. And of course nothing can change the view."

"I was in love with my schoolmistress," my sister offered.

I said, "Don't make fun of me. This is *serious*."

"That was serious, too," said Cécile. "I tried to kill myself."

"How old were you?" I asked.

"What difference does that make?" my sister replied.

"*I* don't remember anything about it," I said. "Which one was she?"

My sister grabbed a cucumber and began slicing it as if she were a *moulinette*.

"If you really want to know she was the one who has the lottery concession at the corner of Saint Mark's now," said my sister.

"The humpback!" I cried.

"She wasn't humpbacked," said Cécile. "One shoulder was higher than the other, that's all."

"We used to call her Madame Brie," I said. "Or was it Madame Pont l'Eveque?"

"Well, it doesn't matter," said Cécile. "I loved her."

A few months ago Cécile borrowed some money from father and opened a shop in the Place de l'Église.

She took three of four pieces of furniture and rubbed them down by hand and already she was making twice as much money as Jean-Loup.

The day I went to see her she was wearing a bracelet from one of father's precious boxes.

"Did you buy it?" I asked.

She said, "He gave me a couple of weeks to make up my mind."

I said, "Who helps you with repairs and moving?"

"A *bonhomme*," she said.

I said, "You don't have to blush."

My sister said, "I know. I wouldn't blush if you had said 'Who are you sleeping with?'"

I said, "Who are you sleeping with?"

My sister said, "A *bonhomme*," still blushing.

Besides the bracelet, she had had stripes put in her hair and bought a little car that she kept shined up like her furniture.

"You know, we didn't have such a bad childhood," I said. "Our parents loved us and we've always gotten

along all right together."

"We never had any *other* friends," said Cécile. "And I used to hate you for living in Paris with things that had to be counted or sent out once a year or rolled in napthaline."

I thought she might have offered to drive me to the station with her little car.

I suppose she was expecting *him* whoever he might be.

Dolly went to the Ninth Congress of Natural Farming and Magali came to stay with us bringing Mouser and a tulle nightgown from her grandmother.

"*I* want a tulle nightgown," said Laure.

I found the nightgown Gérard gave me for our last anniversary and cut off the bottom.

"In that case I'll put my pajamas on," said Magali.

At eleven o'clock Magali woke me to say the hot water bottle had come open.

"*What* hot water bottle?" I asked.

"The one my grandmother sent me, of course," said Magali.

At two o'clock Magali woke me up to say good-bye.

I said, "But you can't go home all by yourself, Magali. Anything might happen!"

"That's what *I* was thinking . . ." said Magali.

51

Dolly came back with an Irish Korean named Patrick Hô.

Useless to tell myself all Chinamen look alike. This one is special.

Passing Patrick Hô on the staircase is like passing their unmade bed.

Eyes, lips, chin — all intimate objects from their life together.

Dolly is lovely in her new hippy outfit, but not very distinguished, I'm afraid. I mistake every slender back on the Boulevard St. Germain for hers.

I select a psychiatrist on the 63 bus route and invent a friend who recommended him, but his secretary is more than happy to give me an appointment without hearing it.

A sign on the psychiatrist's lift says, "Out of order." Like the sign on the lift the first time I went to see Gérard's mother.

The stairs are wider, though, and instead of sweating I am shivering.

Three of Doctor Moreau's waiting room walls are covered by scenes representing the life of Paul and Virginia.

The fourth is unfinished and I make a guess it never will be because they have all begun to peel.

On the table are *Constellation, Le Livre de la Jungle, La Vie Culturelle en Tchecoslavaquie* and two folders entitled *La Vie Familiale #6* and *#14* respectively.

I am about to take a seat beside a baseball when the doctor beckons me into his office, which is filled with unruly geraniums.

"Do you have a boy or girl?" he wants to know.

"Girl," I say demurely pressing my knees together.

"Age?"

"Just turned seven," I simper.

"What diseases?"

"*I'm* the one with the disease," I snap.

When I come to the end of my recital he writes the name of a colleague and hands it to me.

(He himself turns out to be a child specialist.)

Doctor Elaine Ternisin lives on one of those crooked streets that used to be infested with Arabs and are now so expensive.

I open a plate glass door that leads through a newly restored medieval garden and up a circular staircase smelling of beeswax to where a lady in horn-rimmed glasses sits at a refectory table gleaming like the ones in my sister's new boutique.

In one hand she is holding a paperweight and on the third finger of the other she wears a gold and enamel snake.

"You were sent by Docteur Dupré," she tells me.

When I do not deny it she beckons to someone in the wings.

It turns out to be another lady, also wearing horn-rimmed glasses, but younger with nice breasts.

I look at her left hand.

Sure enough she is wearing an enamel serpent, as well.

"Give Madame a clean blotter and bring one of the forms in the lower file," Doctor Ternisin says.

"Never mind, I just came to say I can't come to-day," I say.

"When would you like us to set up another appointment?" the doctor asks.

"Never," I bravely conclude.

I pulled open the bedroom door and found Gérard leaning over a box from which Magali's voice cried, "Hold him!"

For a moment I didn't understand what was going on then I began shouting, "You're *monstrous! Monstrous!*"

Gérard looked surprised.

"I just ran a wire to the inter-com to see if it was working," he said. "It's not the reason I installed it."

"Then why are you sitting there?" I cried.

Gérard said, "I don't know. There's never anything good on TV. Anyway all they were talking about was cutting the cat's claws."

"How do you work the dials?" I ask.

"First turn on this," said Gérard, "then keep trying the buttons until you find the room they're in."

I admired the way his fingers moved so nimbly from one button to the other. Covering his hand with mine I pulled him quickly to me.

While we were bumping up and down on the bed I could hear Magali, still anxious, and Dolly's whispery replies.

By keeping tuned in continuously I found that Dolly imitated pop singers when she was alone and became so terrified of mentioning it I no longer dared to see her.

When the inter-com died of its own accord it was like a present.

Yesterday Maria forgot to put out the trash so I took it down and found Patrick Hô tinkering with his motorcycle.

He had a knapsack and a roadmap beside him.

"Are you going for a trip?" I asked, hoping he wouldn't notice how my heart was beating.

He kissed me hard, wrenching my neck and painfully squeezing my buttocks.

His lips still tasted of Dolly!

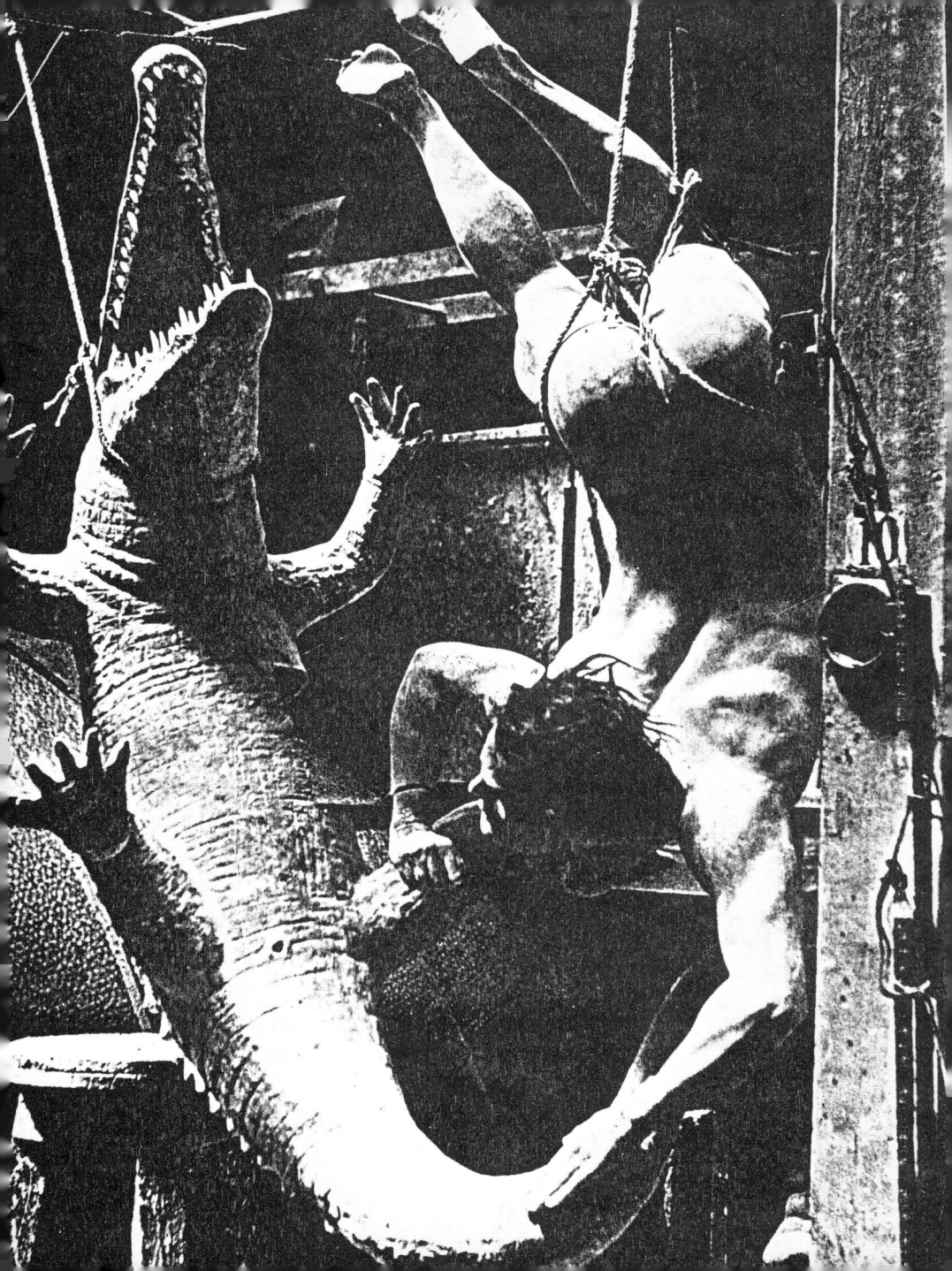

This afternoon Dolly and I took the children to see a play based on the adventures of Jacques Cousteau.

She had painted her eyelids pale purple and put tiny spots of rouge on each cheekbone leaving her mouth naked.

Several trapped fathers looked at her, but for once she didn't look back and in the dark I found her hand and kept it through the coming events and half the feature.

The door bell rang this morning and there was Cécile.

In one hand she had an old valise and in the other a straw basket about the size of a walnut containing dried flowers and a china poodle.

"Do you recognize that?" she asked.

"Of course," I said. "It's Mama's poodle before the last. Why didn't you give it to *her*?"

"I don't know," said Cécile. "Because she annoys me, I suppose. And because I was afraid of making her sad after he was run over."

As she arranged her brush and comb on Gérard's desk and hung her dressing gown on a hook behind the door I realized she was pregnant.

"Does it show badly?" she asked.

"You have blue circles under your eyes and your breasts are pointy," I said.

"I have an address," she said, rummaging in her handbag.

We went into the kitchen and made orange leaf tea and drank two cups the way we used to do when we were worried about examinations.

Cécile was in bed for two days, eating Alpine Mints and letting down her hems.

The minute Gérard left for work we would begin talking and as soon as he and Laure were asleep we started in again.

I even resented it when Dolly came and stretched out on the foot of the bed.

"Attention!" said Cécile. "Your Dolly's a firefly. She'll lead you into trouble, if you don't crush her by mistake."

"And she isn't even pretty," I marveled resentfully.

"With a face like hers why should she bother?" replied my sister.

I said, "I love you, Cécile. I've always loved you. Sometimes at night I miss you so beside me. And the field of goldenrod that used to give you hay fever. Do you remember the red-haired man who came to see father every Saturday? Was he mother's lover? Is it true Laure is a snob? Why did you encourage me to marry Gérard, I was in love with someone else. Really in love. I think of him to this day."

Cécile said, "Stop trying to go back to old days. You did everything the way you wanted to. You've

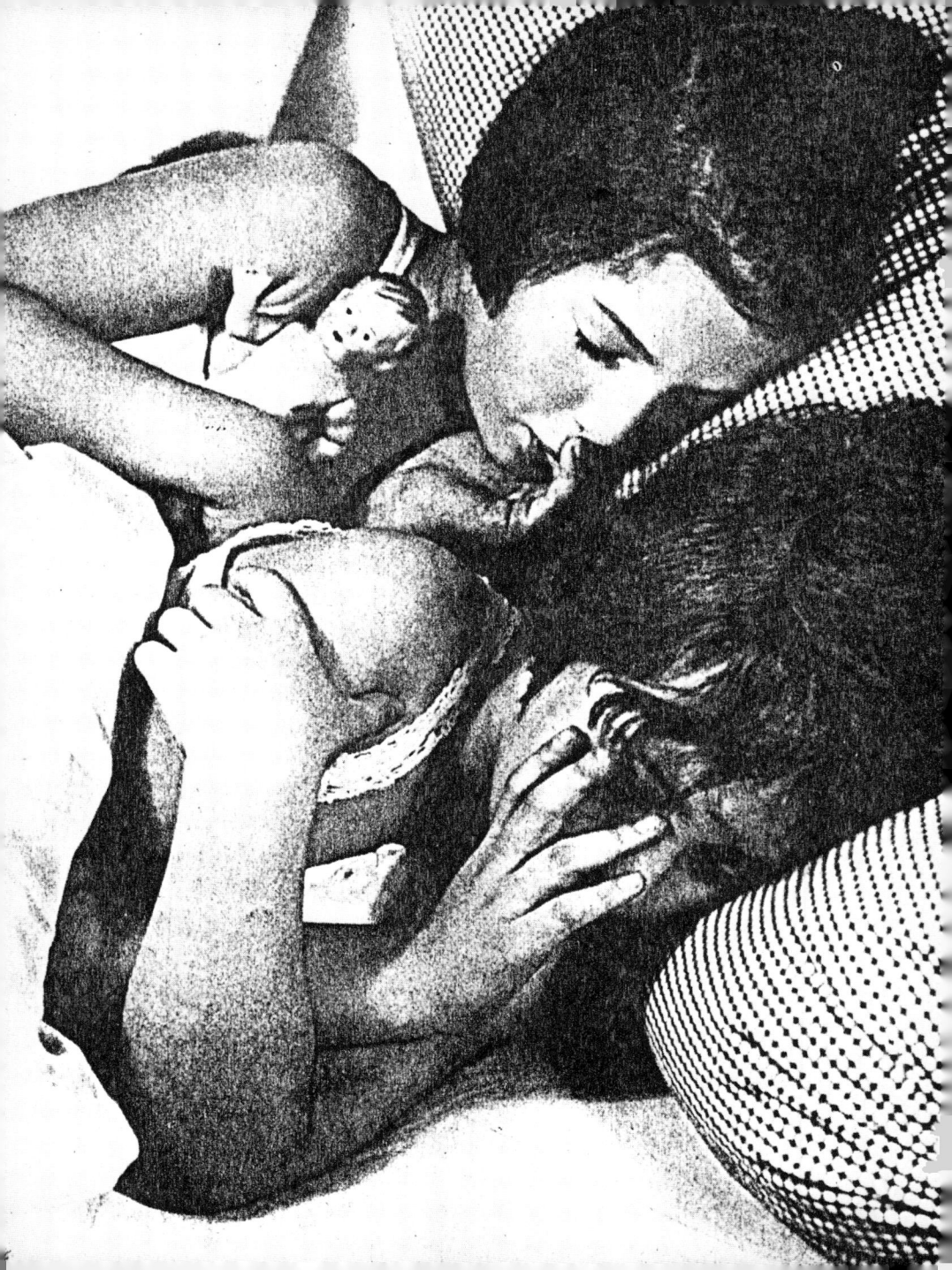

always done things the way you wanted to. Hand me the aspirin tablets. No, I'm not in pain, I just like to take aspirin tablets. You were nice to your mother-in-law. You said so yourself. Think of that if you have to think back. Now let me sleep."

"And you aren't sorry?" I pleaded.

"About what?"

"About the *baby*."

"I'm sorry about the money," said Cécile. "I was going to have the bags taken out from under my eyes."

Before going to bed I looked at my own eyes.

They seemed all right, but it was true I looked younger if I pulled the lids to the side. Also a bit like Patrick Hô.

Usually when we go to Melun for the weekend Laure takes along a friend.

This time it is Mariette Archimèdes, the daughter of her math prof.

She is plump and slow and Laure feels glamorous beside her.

She is also blonder than Laure, but in this they league together to be two little blonde girls with hair the same length.

It has turned icy spring with mud everywhere.

I went for a walk in the woods and when I got back the girls were sitting in the same place in front of the empty fireplace not even sewing doll's clothes.

If Dolly were here I would start a fire and make a soufflé with the leftover chicken.

I may anyway.

The thought that we must spend another night here is intolerable.

Poor Gérard! He must have been suffering that night we took the furniture to Joigny. Still it's better to have lost than never to have had anything except impossible dreams.

I was helping Dolly make sachets out of orange rinds and cloves when a young priest from St. Thomas Aquinas came to the door.

I thought he was a little embarrassed by Dolly's shorts and bare feet, but he took the cigarette and the sherry she offered.

Most of our conversation was about the difficulty of getting young people into the church and how women like us were needed to encourage them.

When Gérard and I were first married we sometimes went to church but since his mother's funeral I haven't been in one. I don't suppose Gérard has either, though you don't know everything, as witness the way his affair with Mademoiselle Dreux was almost over before I even suspected it.

When the priest was gone Dolly said, "I'll go to his get-together. Will you?"

I said, "No, he'd keep coming around for things."

Dolly said, "I wouldn't mind that."

To change the subject I asked if she ever joined one of those communes in California.

Dolly said, "You can be as bored with twenty people as you can with two."

"I'd never get bored with *you*," I said, expecting her not to notice but she said, "You already are a little. You used to try to get Laure to drink carrot juice to be like Magali. Now you don't care."

"Carrot juice!" I said.

"Yes, carrot juice," said Dolly.

I suppose my sister would let me know call if she weren't well.

On the other hand she nearly died of appendicitis because she didn't want to tell anyone it hurt.

"What will Laure say when she finds out about her grandfather?" she once asked me.

I was always proud of our parents. I never called father an *antiquaire* the way she did.

Yesterday a window washer started work on the windows of the apartment building opposite.

I was wondering if it would be impolite to call across and ask him to come to us later when he set his bucket down and rolled himself over the parapet.

A bystander rushed into the café next door, probably to use the telephone, and another brought a blanket from the laundramat.

Just before the ambulance arrived the priest who had come to see Dolly gave last rites.

When Gérard came home I told him about it, but he was not very interested.

When Dolly gets back from her tour of the Châteaux de la Loire I can tell about seeing her priest.

Of course, it's ridiculous to imagine it would have changed things if I had spoken.

93

Does anything really change anything?

I slipped my wedding ring off and laid it in the spice rack while I was helping Maria polish the silver.

Later I noticed I had forgotten to put it back on and decided to leave it off until Gérard noticed.

When we went to bed he still hadn't said anything.

Chantal invited me to lunch in Neuilly.

She had avocado with baby shrimps like in America and afterwards she showed me some silk slips she had had made.

I didn't know people still wore slips, let alone have them made.

Her jungle plant has grown all the way up the stairs to the children's rooms which have pictures of Alain Delon and Fred Astaire on the walls.

I was reminded that Michel would have been thirteen in a few days. (A little younger than her Théo.)

"Sometimes I think of moving closer to the center of town, but I am so used to the space and the air," Chantal said.

As we were having coffee she said, "I suppose you see François and Maryse. I have never reproached Maryse. After all, I left François to shift for himself the whole of Easter week. But Maryse deserves a better life—always working even though François is doing so well."

Usually I say, "Maybe she likes working."

This time I said, "Why don't *you* work? You could get a job showing apartments and drive your car around in the afternoons."

Chantal said, "Why don't *you?*"

This evening I asked Gérard if he ever thought of selling the house at Melun and buying farther out now that people have begun building around us.

Gérard said, "The drive would take too long. Don't you *like* our house in Melun?"

It was bound to happen.

The blue eyed delivery boy from the delicatessen took an order to Dolly this morning and didn't leave till noon.

"Never mind," said Cécile. "Soon you'll laugh about it."

"Did *you*?" I asked.

"Of course," said Cécile.

"You told me you wanted to kill yourself," I said.

"So?"

In a loose blouse she was sanding down a refectory table. She never looked healthier or happier.

"Come meet my new partner," she said.

Ariane was married to Docteur Zhendre who owned the Clinique on the Grande rue.

She used to be Ariane Cordet and her father was a notary.

We never knew her, of course. She belonged to the group that went to Paris on weekends and skied at mid-terms.

When she saw me she cried, "Genviève!" and kissed me on both cheeks.

At the café she ordered a 'gros rouge' and she and my sister alternately stood the rounds.

"*Voilà tout*," she said after every story she told.

"*Ma cocotte*" was what she called my sister.

"No reason to tell father I came out to see you," I said.

My sister, who was now cooking a marlin, said, "What's the point? Secrets always get around."

"You must have thought *your* secret was safe in Paris!" I said.

My sister said, "I hoped so, but I was wrong."

"What happened?" I asked.

"He was angry," said Cécile. "Another baby would have tied me to the house for another year. And then he feels it especially because they always look like him."

"Maybe this one wouldn't have!" I said.

By the way my sister looked at me I could tell I had said something stupid.

Outside Jean-Loup was leaning against the fence picking his teeth though he had not yet eaten.

He said, *"Alors, ça va la petite?"*

I said, *"Ça va. Et toi?"*

"Ça va, ça va . . ."

The children, who had returned through the field carrying milk, now began playing a game of catch.

My sister is right — they do look like him.

Before I returned to Paris I crossed the river to dine with my mother and father.

Maman was getting a chill and papa was expecting someone from the Louvre.

"I'll make a soubise," I said.

Maman said, "Do as you wish. I'm going to drift off for a minute on this couch, if it will hold me."

As I mixed the sauce tears ran down my cheeks.

As always the house smelled of mould and leather, liniment, powder of anise and onions and earth from the root cellar and things long gone from the numerous empty drawers around us such as newspaper clippings, old photographs and broken vases, parts of trophies from Africa, tobacco and pin cushions and documents. As well as rotted rubber.

"Come look at these drawings," said my father uncorking the pear brandy. "I found them in a portfolio I bought at La Verrière last week."

Here was a series of carefully drawn views of the Champs Elysées grown wild with cherry trees and a watercolor of a woman with an umbrella standing so that her naked bottom was reflected in a puddle.

"They're interesting," I said. "Maybe a taxi driver in his spare time. Or a retired person."

My father laughed loudly.

Later I noticed the initials in the corner were the same as his.

A coincidence, surely.

It was cold and starry.

As the two of us stood at the head of the stoop my father suddenly said, "Your mother wants us to buy a house in Vence."

"Then you could stock smaller things and sell to tourists," I began cautiously.

At that moment the telephone rang and my father pushed past me without bothering to say goodnight.

I used to think of him as putting up with those calls from Paris.

That's how much *I* knew!

On the train back to Paris I sat opposite a couple carrying a cat with the same markings as Mouser, though its features were different. (Whereas Mouser had a square head with bundles of sturdy whiskers, this one had a pointed face and dainty paws that he kept licking.)

Nevertheless I said, "I know someone who brought a cat just like that from America," to which the woman replied, "Ooooooh *him*! He doesn't like travelling. All you have to do is show him the leash and he hides under the table, but what can I do? My twin lives in Garches and she has a heart condition. I have to go down there sometimes, don't I?"

As I was tucking Laure in she put on a saccharine expression and said, "Are you happy to be home, *petite maman?*"

I could as easily have nodded my head. There was certainly no reason for saying, "Let me think about it."

I've made up my mind not to see Dolly again.

108

After all, it isn't as if I were giving anything up. There's nothing for me whether I see her or not.

After dinner I swallowed a cognac and raced downstairs.

Boris opened the door holding a bottle of champagne.

"Come have a drink while Dolly is dressing," he said.

In the living room Magali lay on the carpet with her feet in a chair.

She said, "Oh I have such a headache, you can't imagine!"

"Have it somewhere else," said Boris.

She gave him a pitying look and slunk down the hall.

After the first two glasses of champagne I felt as if I owed Boris a debt so I said,

"Naturally you know Dolly has lovers."

Boris said, "Well, that's nice. I was afraid she was denying herself while I was out philandering. Excuse me while I open another bottle of this stuff."

When he came back he had Dolly with him.

"You look glum," she said. "Let Boris fill your glass."

I said, "I'll let Boris do anything he wants to do. Boris and I are friends. Maybe we could be more than that, what do you think, Boris?"

Boris said, "Dolly, turn your back please while Genviève and I become more than friends."

Dolly said, "I want to be more than friends, *too*. Why don't you go back upstairs and get your husband?"

I threw my glass in the fireplace Russian style and wobbled out to the hall.

Dolly opened the door smelling of baby powder and painted like a new croquet post.

"You're beautiful, Dolly," I said. "Really beautiful. Forgive me for taking so long to know it."

She said, "I'm glad you think so. I think you're despicable."

"But *why?*" I wanted to know. "Must we always live in our boxes like hamsters? Can't we ever say what we feel? I'm tired of loving you and not even knowing what to propose. Where is my steam iron? When you borrow things you could at least tell me about it . . ."

I thought I was keeping my voice low and reasonable, but apparently not because here came Gérard running down the stairs and led me into the elevator.

"Lie down while I make coffee," Gérard said.

"But I want to help you!" I said. "I've never done anything for you, even bring up your son. I love you even if I love Dolly better. I love everyone. I would even have loved your grandfather who made cough syrup if I had known him."

Seeing my pleas were no good I went to the desk and got out the Japanese letter opener Gérard's sister gave us for our marriage and stuck it into my wrist.

It was quite easy. Much easier than I would have guessed from cutting up chickens, and less disgusting.

When Gérard returned the blood was gushing neatly into a silver bread basket we used sometimes when my mother-in-law was alive.

I made that up, of course.

Actually I went straight to bed and woke up without even a hangover.

In the end Dolly and I lived together for nearly a year and during that time I never for a minute ceased being jealous, even when we were lying breast to breast beneath her leopard patterned sheets. For Dolly was indeed a firefly and not the many chambered Nautilus I had been led to believe.

Still, we had our happiness. Mostly the sort we had known at Zermatt when our eyes met and agreed on ten more minutes of guessing games before putting the children to bed or swore allegiance against bubble gum.

(Two ladies behind plate glass . . .)

MAMAN... NE M'ABANDONNE PAS...

ADMINISTRATION GÉNÉRALE DE L'ASSISTANCE PUBLIQUE À PARIS

AVIS

AUX PERSONNES AYANT L'INTENTION D'ABANDONNER LEURS ENFANT

CONSÉQUENCES
de l'abandon d'un enfant

MOYENS D'ÉVITER
l'abandon d'un enfant

You may be surprised that Gérard allowed me to carry on this way on the very site of his own lost *bonheur*, but to be frank, if Boris didn't object there wasn't much Gérard could do without bringing matters into the open. An idea that would not have occurred to him.

Only Laure refused to be a party to our goings on, cleaving first to the maid then to Chantal who had taken to dropping around to give Gérard a hand.

What happened in the end was simply that Boris moved his headquarters to Rome and with him went my Dolly. Dressed in a sky blue sari printed with tiny flowers, very detailed as though viewed beneath a magnifying glass, her glossy hair held back by a broken shoestring.

I had come home carrying the first asparagus of the season and found Dolly in a sea of shawls, necker-chiefs, handbags, venetian glass beads and unbegun needlepoint, lining her suitcases with multi-colored paper.

"But *why*?" I wanted to know as usual. "*I* can work, Dolly. I *want* to. We can get a place on the Ile St. Louis when the lease runs out. We could even take a house in Villeneuve and keep rabbits."

Dolly pulled a plastic bag over her head and looked at me through the two e's in *Shirtee*, a boutique she favored on the rue du Bac.

"Oh that would be so lovely!" she sighed.

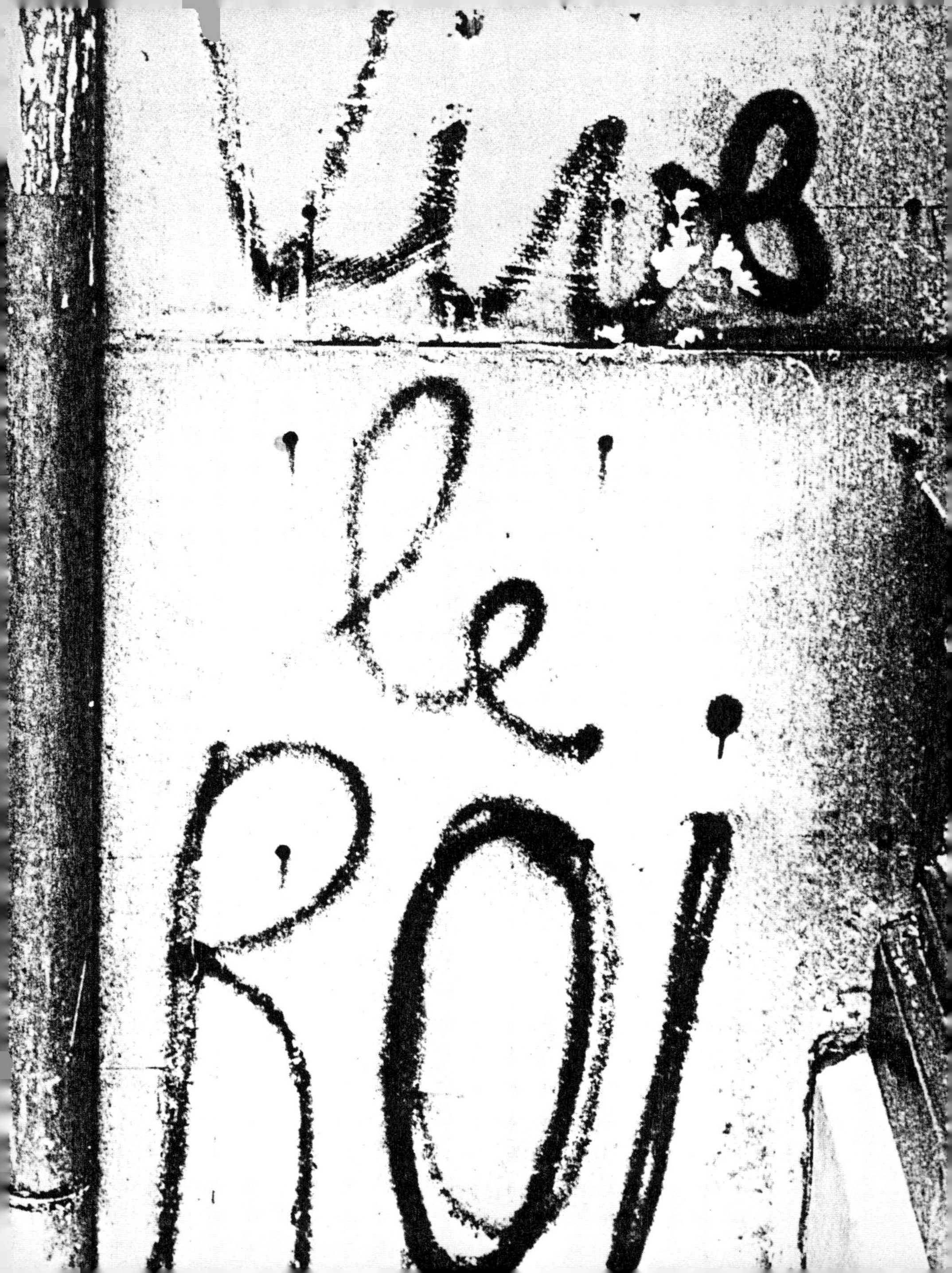
Vive
le
Roi

Alas, it wasn't for practical reasons that Dolly was leaving.

She simply wished to be with Boris. Piling up his mail in the hall. Forgetting to take his suits to the cleaners.

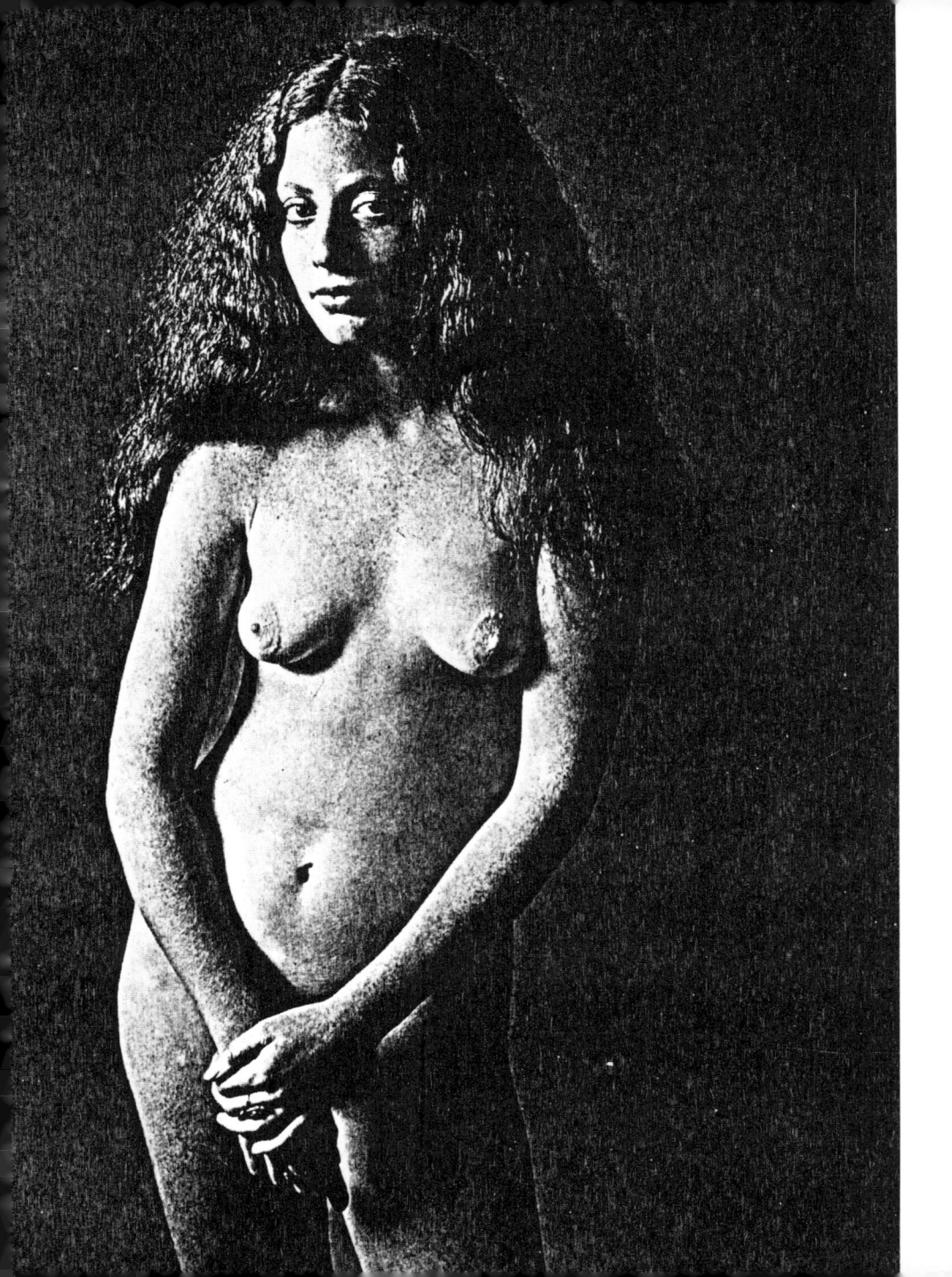

It wasn't fair, I told myself. They had themselves, why did they need each other?

Anyway, what was so great about Boris?

The times we were all together he was far from being as forceful a lover as I suspected Patrick Hô might have been, though I liked the soft hair on his chest and a few little tricks he showed me.

I felt somewhat bitter about losing Gérard, too.

He had been a good provider and I should never have left him to go off to Zermatt. Or perhaps I should have allowed him to tell me about Mademoiselle Dreux the way he wanted to. Or not married.

To tell the truth I was never so good at pinpointing things as Chantal.

At first the idea of taking a job with Dolly gone seemed so ridiculous I could hardly keep my mind on the ads. Then I started asking questions for an insurance company and I enjoyed it.

I was quite good at it, too. I would have been up for a raise if I hadn't gotten bored and begun to ask questions of my own.

Now I've taken to the road selling unbreakable baking dishes.

Weekends I take Laure to the movies if I'm in the city. That way we don't have to talk, and afterwards Chantal and Gérard invite me to dinner.

They have transformed the two apartments into a handsome duplex but they are selling it because, in the end, Neuilly really suits them better.

Chantal and Laure get on wonderfully.

Chantal teaches her all the womanly arts—sewing, piano, how to tell mink from muskrat, etc.

There is scarcely a minute when they are not exchanging little gestures of affection which they try to hide, perhaps to keep from causing me pain.

Gérard seems to like the boys, too. At least he has the youngest enrolled at Pershing Hall and the other is making a tour of American capitols on his next vacation.

"So what more can you ask?" asks my sister who, together with Ariane, has opened still another shop and will buy father out when he leaves this fall. (The stock, that is. The house itself will be made into a gasoline station.)

Actually, more (or even less) is not quite the point.

I just want *Dolly*. (And Magali and Mouser, if you insist.)

Last night I dreamed I received a card from them saying "bother" or "lather". Or maybe it was "blotter".

It doesn't matter.

I woke up in tears again.

Today, crossing the rue de la République in Dijon, I saw a goldfish run over by a bicycle.

One minute it was swimming calmly in its transparent bubble, suspended from its owner's finger by a loop of twine, the next minute the twine broke and what will you? I continued on toward Arles.

I don't think the bicyclist even noticed.

Tomorrow I'll likely sleep in Marseille. Or maybe I'll stay where I am. Who knows, anything can happen.

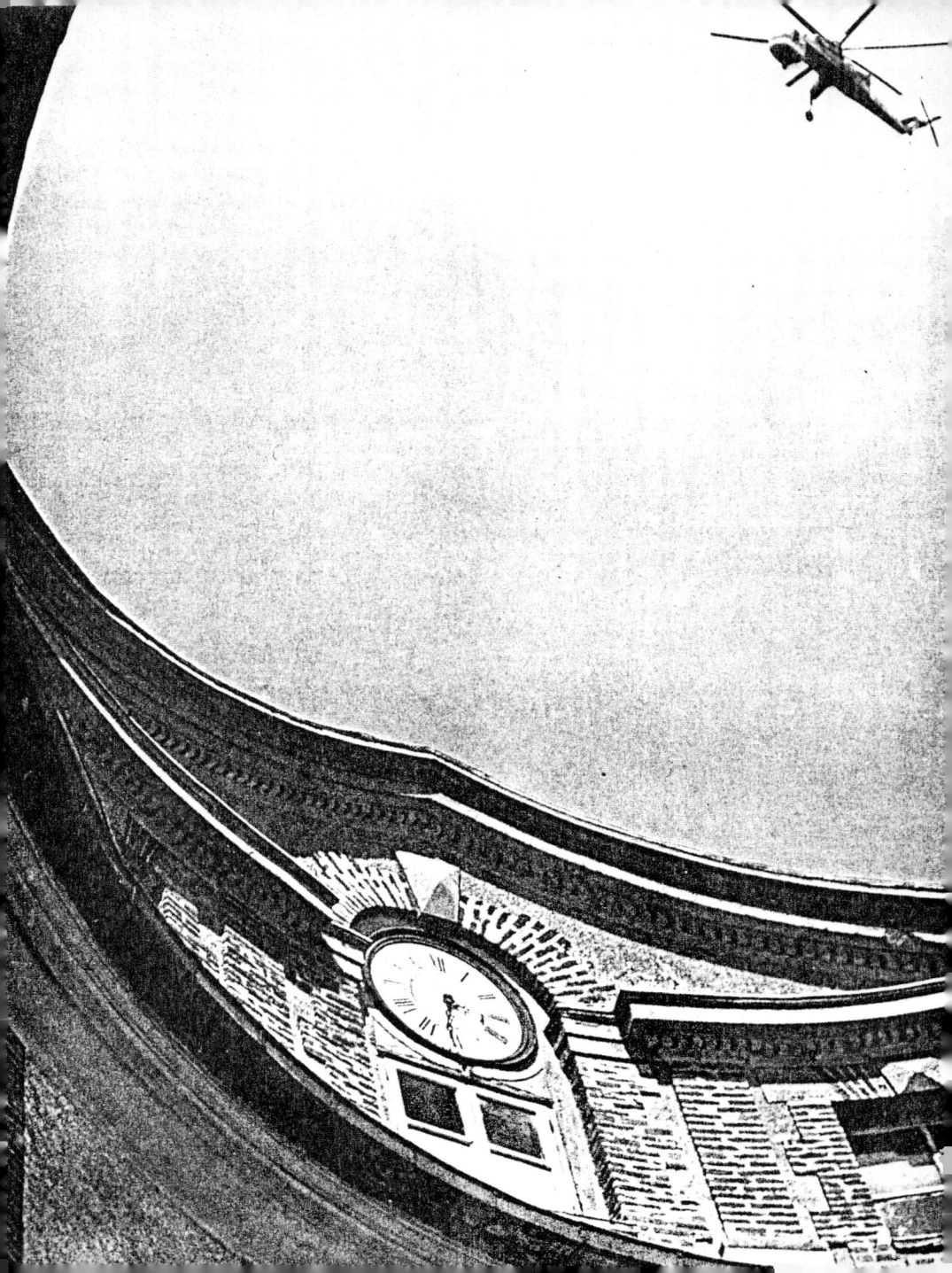

Anything!

Photographs

Pati Hill was born in Kentucky and lives in France with her husband, Paul Bianchini, and their daughter, Paola.